Chocolate Island

Karen Dolby

Illustrated by Caroline Church

Series Editor: Gaby Waters
Assistant Editor: Michelle Bates

D1347872

Contents

About this Book

This book is about Tom and Grace and their amazing adventures on Chocolate Island. It all begins one day when they spot a poster for a chocolate cake baking competition . . .

Chunkies Chocolate Cakes and Cookies Competition

to bake the best ever Chocolate Cake

Sensational prizes:
World fame as a cook. Television appearances. Lifetime's supply of chocolate cakes and cookies.

Turn the page for [gr]eat adventure and solve [th]e puzzles along the way.

Keep your eyes open for clues. If you get stuck there are answers on pages 31 and 32.

Chunkies Chocolate
Cakes and Cookies
Competition

to bake the best ever
Chocolate Cake

Sensational prizes:

World fame as a cook. Television
appearances. Lifetime's supply of
chocolate cakes and cookies.

Chocolate Cake Baking Competition

When Tom and Grace saw the Chunkies Cake Baking
Competition poster they were very excited. Their Great
Uncle Ollie baked the yummiest chocolate cakes and
they were sure he could win the prize.

"Think of all the chocolate we could win," said Grace.

"And we could appear on TV with Uncle Ollie - we'd be famous," added Tom.

They raced to Uncle Ollie's house. "We want you to make a chocolate cake - your best ever," exclaimed Tom, waving the competition leaflet at his Uncle.

"I'm afraid I can't see a thing without my spectacles," Ollie said. "And I seem to have lost them. I was sorting through this old chest when I last saw them."

Can you spot Uncle Ollie's spectacles?

Mrs.
Nougat

Granny
Truffle

Young
Ollie

Chocolate
Island

Chocolate
Well

Granny Truffle's Story

Uncle Ollie sighed. "I've no chance with Mrs. Nougat around. She always wins competitions and her chocolate cake is famous."

Tom and Grace shuddered. "Mrs. Nougat ~ yuck! She's horrible and everyone says she cheats."

Uncle Ollie sighed. "My Granny Truffle made THE best chocolate cake. Now, if I had her recipe and some Chocolate Island chocolate, then my cake would be a winner. My Granny used to tell me stories about a fantastic island with a chocolate well, chocolate drop trees, and chocolate fudge streams."

"Just imagine the most deliciously yummy chocolate anyone has ever tasted, bubbling up from the ground. I used to have dreams about the island, wishing and wishing I could go there. A long time ago now . . ."

"And did you ever go there?" asked Tom.

"Oh no," smiled Ollie, mysteriously. "Although Granny did draw me a map showing where the island is. It's here somewhere. It's easy to spot because it has the Chocolate Island symbol of a moon and star in the corner."

Can you see the Chocolate Island map?

The Old Map

Grace and Tom lifted out the old map.
As they looked at it, they decided they
MUST visit Chocolate Island.

If Uncle Ollie was going to bake the winning chocolate cake and beat ghastly Mrs. Nougat, it was up to them to find the special Chocolate Island chocolate for him.

Which do you think is Chocolate Island? (Look for its sign.)

Aboard the Chocolate Queen

They dashed down to the seashore where a strange old boat was bobbing up and down in the waves, ready to set sail. Captain Cook welcomed them aboard.

"Hold tight for the journey of a lifetime," she laughed. And they were off. Wizzz! Wooosh! Wooo!

It felt as if they were flying. But they zoomed along at such a pace it was hard to tell. The boat slowed.

"Chocolate Island ahoy!" Their Captain shouted.

Tom leaned over the side, eager to catch his first glimpse of Chocolate Island. But which one was it? Soon Tom spotted a chocolate fudge stream, chocolate drop trees and chocolate pebbles on the beach.

Can you find all the things Tom spotted? How many pebbles can you count?

Chocolate Island

Captain Cook handed Grace a small purse when they landed. "These are Chocolate Island pennies," she said. "Watch out for the sinking syrup and galoptious gloop! And never believe anything the whistling candy trees tell you."

Grace and Tom wondered what kind of place the island was . . . They were about to find out.

Hello! I'm a Chocolate Island guide. Try some rainbow drops, they're tasty.

They saw chocolate everywhere ~ milk chocolate apples, white chocolate peaches and dark chocolate chestnuts, growing next to real fruit and nuts.

This is Hansel and Gretel's house. They get a bit cross when too many people start nibbling pieces.

"I have to go now," said the guide. "Tiggy will help you find the chocolate well. He's under the tutti frutti tree with chocolate pears and white flowers growing on it."

Can you see Tiggy beneath the tutti frutti tree?

The Chocolate Chip Mine

Lying beneath the tree was Tiggy, a sleepy-looking tiger.

"You're looking for the chocolate well?" he yawned.
"Visit the chocolate chip mine first. It's the only one
of its kind. You can't visit the island and not
see it."

A talking tiger! It was hard to believe.
He led them to a small red cable
car at the top of the mine shaft.

"I must finish my snooze
now," said Tiggy. "After the
mine, you should go to
the waterfalls."

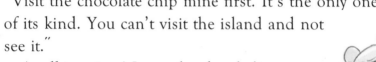

The cable car rushed down and down. PLING! A bell rang as they hit the bottom. They were in a lofty, brightly lit cavern. On all sides miners were chipping away at the chocolate chunks in the rock. The chips were whisked away to be baked into cookies. Grace wondered how many miners there were.

How many chocolate miners can you see?

Chocolate Falls

When they clambered out of the cable car, Tom and Grace saw the waterfalls ahead. But these were no ordinary falls.

"They look like chocolate milkshake," exclaimed Grace, as she watched the foaming, bubbling liquid tumbling over the rocks.

Tom scrambled down to the rainbow tinted pool at the bottom. "I'm going for a swim," he called, jumping in.

Soon, Grace and Tom were splashing, leaping and diving. As Grace came up for air, she found herself staring into the unblinking eyes of the largest toad she had ever seen. The toad stopped munching chocolate beans and began croaking loudly. It seemed impossible, but it was giving them a message.

What is the toad's message?

Inside the Cookie Café

"This place is bound to be crammed with scrumptious things to eat," said Tom, at the door to the Cookie Café. He wasn't disappointed. He licked his lips at all the amazing goodies. When the other customers heard the children's quest to find the well, they tried to help.

Buy your copy of Granny Truffle's Recipe Book HERE 12 CI Pennies

Granny Truffle

Turn left outside the café.

Follow the crispy crackle path over the chocolate brick bridge to the signpost.

Just as they were about to leave, Grace noticed something. "Remember Granny Truffle? I've just spotted something that Uncle Ollie would find very useful. Luckily I still have those Chocolate Island pennies we were given."

Can you see what Grace has spotted?

The signpost will point you to the Toffee Tower.

The chocolate well is in the middle of a tricky maze.

Climb the Tower to find your way through the maze to the chocolate well.

Chunky Chocolate Signpost

Outside the café, Grace and Tom turned left along the
crispy crackle path. "It's made from chocolate crispies,"
exclaimed Grace, breaking off a small piece to eat. It
was sweet and crunchy.

But Tom was too busy staring at the stream. It was easy
to see why it was called the Bubbling Brook. It kept
bubbling up into huge balloons which popped loudly.
Soon they turned a corner and saw the chunky chocolate
signpost to the Toffee Tower in from of them.

BUBBLING BROOK

A plump squirrel was perched on top of the post munching. The sign pointed to three paths, but all three pointers had pieces missing. Tom could see the word Toffee on two of them.

He picked up the piece which said Tower. "I know what to do," he said. "We just have to match this piece to one of the pointers. Then we'll know which path to take to the Toffee Tower."

Can you match the broken piece to the sign?

Sinking Syrup

As Tom and Grace started along the path to the Toffee
Tower, the trees grew thicker and thicker. Soon it was very
dark. Tom hurried ahead. Squelch, squelch, schloop! He
seemed to be wading through sticky syrup. Suddenly he was
sinking ~ to his ankles, to his knees, then to his waist.
"Help!" he yelled.

A very strange thing happened next. The red and white
striped candy trees growing on all sides began to whistle
and speak!

"Keep going," they whistled. "Wade to the middle, keep to the golden gloop stones and avoid the mossy green ones." Tom was about to follow their advice when Grace stopped him.

"Wait!" she shouted. "Remember what Captain Cook told us when we first arrived? I know what you have to do."

What did Captain Cook say? What do you think Tom should do?

Mallow Maze

Tom still felt sticky when they arrived at the Toffee Tower. In front of it wound the Mallow Maze and in the middle of that was the chocolate well.

"I'll race you to the top of the Tower," called Tom. "From there we can plot our route through the maze to the chocolate well."

They huffed and puffed their way up to a balcony and looked down.

Can you find a way through the maze to the chocolate well?

The Chocolate Well

"We're here at last," exclaimed Grace, when they reached the well. "I can't wait to try the chocolate."

Together they hauled up the bucket. There was silence as they licked their lips. It really was THE most delicious chocolate they had ever, ever tasted.

But time was running out. They had to get home quickly if Uncle Ollie was to bake his chocolate cake in time for the competition.

They raced back through the maze, past bubbling streams and waterfalls to the beach. But how were they to get home? The ferry was nowhere to be seen. Luckily help was on hand.

What is the time? Is it safe for Grace and Tom to cross the underwater path?

There is an underwater path back to the mainland. It's safe to cross when the water is less than knee deep at low tide.

If there is no ferry you may be able to cross by the underwater path
The water is over your head depth at 8 o'clock
It's shoulder deep at 10 o'clock
Knee deep at 12 o'clock
Ankle deep at 2 o'clock
Toe deep at 4 o'clock

The Competition

Grace and Tom splashed over the watery path, raced across the shore and panted their way back to Uncle Ollie's house.

There was no time to lose. Uncle Ollie happily set to work with scales, pans, mixing bowls, flour, eggs and all the other ingredients that went into Granny Truffle's sensational chocolate cake recipe. Not forgetting the most important of all ~ the Chocolate Island chocolate.

The finished cake looked perfect and smelled delicious. At the Chunkies Chocolate Cake Baking Competition, the judges seemed impressed. Tom nudged Grace as one after the other, the judges came back for second helpings. There WAS someone who did not look too happy at the way the competition was going.

Can you see who it is? Which one do you think is Uncle Ollie's cake?

Prize Giving

There was silence in the hall. The big moment had come. Mr. Chunky, the chief judge, stepped onto the platform.

"Today, there was one chocolate cake beyond compare, one cake which everyone loved," he said. "The winner is . . . Uncle Ollie."

Everyone cheered and clapped. Smiling happily, Uncle Ollie walked up to receive his prize winner's cup with Grace and Tom. He held it high and gave the toast: "To Granny Truffle and Chocolate Island!"

"And the best ever adventure!" added Tom.

Answers

Pages 4-5

Uncle Ollie's spectacles are here.

Pages 6-7

The map is circled here. You can see the moon and star sign in the corner.

Pages 8-9

Chocolate Island is here.

You can see the Chocolate Island symbol of the moon and star on the signpost.

Pages 10-11

This is Chocolate Island.

You can see the chocolate fudge stream and chocolate drop trees marked here. There are twelve chocolate pebbles on the beach.

Pages 12-13

You can see Tiggy here under the tutti frutti tree.

Pages 14-15

There are eleven chocolate chip miners. You can see them all circled here.

Pages 16-17

The message is:
GO TO THE
COOKIE CAFÉ

Pages 18-19

Grace has spotted a sign for Granny Truffle's Chocolate Recipe Book. They can use the Chocolate Island pennies that Captain Cook gave them to buy a copy.

Pages 20-21

The broken piece which says Tower matches this pointer. Grace and Tom must take this path to the Toffee Tower.

Pages 22-23

Captain Cook told them to:"Watch out for the sinking syrup and galoptious gloop. And never believe anything the whistling candy trees tell you." (See page 12.) Grace knows that Tom should not do what the trees are telling him. To cross the syrup he must only walk on the green stones and avoid the gloop stones.

Pages 24-25

The route through the maze is marked here in red.

Pages 26-27

The clock on the Toffee Tower shows the time is 2:30 and the signpost tells them the water is less than ankle deep at that time. This means it is safe for Grace and Tom to cross the causeway back to the mainland and home.

Pages 28-29

Mrs. Nougat is not very happy. You can recognize her from page 6. Ollie's cake has the Chocolate Island moon and star sign as decoration.

Mrs. Nougat

Ollie's cake

By the way . . . did you spot Captain Cook appearing throughout the story? You can see her on page 4 at the shop window; on pages 10 and 12 with her boat; helping Tom and Grace on page 27; and as one of the judges on page 29.

This edition first published in 2002 by Usborne Publishing Ltd., Usborne House, 83-85 Saffron Hill, London EC1N 8RT, England. www.usborne.com Copyright © 2002, 1995 Usborne Publishing Ltd. The name Usborne and the devices ♀ 🌐 are Trade Marks of Usborne Publishing Ltd. All rights reserved.